Josie's New Coat

Monica Hughes

Illustrated by Lisa Smith

Josie and Mum went out.
They went to get a new coat
for Josie.

"Can I have a red coat
or a fluffy coat?" said Josie.

Josie and Mum went to look
at the coats.
Mum looked at some red coats.
Josie looked at some fluffy coats.

Josie saw a fluffy coat.

"I like it!" said Josie.

"I like it too," said Mum,

"but it's too big.

All the fluffy coats are too big."

Josie saw a red coat.

"I like it!" said Josie.

"I like it too," said Mum,

"but it's too little.

All the red coats are too little."

"So I can't have a fluffy coat,"
said Josie.
"And I can't have a red coat."

Then Mum saw some red and
blue and yellow coats.
"Look at these coats, Josie,"
said Mum.
Josie put on a coat.

"I like it!" said Mum.

"Do you like it, Josie?"

Josie said, "Y-Y-Y-Yes."

Mum said, "We will take this coat."

Josie went to school
in her new coat.

She saw Ravi and Tilly.

"I've got a new coat!" said Josie.

"So have I!" said Ravi.

"So have I!" said Tilly.